P9-CNI-863

# Sammy on . . .

*death of the family dog:*
When Giles died, I expected a miracle. I walked in the front door after school and asked, "Is Giles still dead?"

*Grandmama Welty:*
My friend Amos said he thought Grandmama was old and creepy. It worried me that people liked you better when you were young.

*cheating at school:*
I began to wonder whether I was plain bad to the core.

*divorce:*
I asked my father if he thought he was ever going to get divorced and he said no, at least not in the next few weeks, because he was busy with other things. . . .

*the neighbor's suicide:*
I didn't go to sleep right away that night, but I didn't creep out of bed either. If boys like Michael could just die as easy as that, I thought I'd better stay put right where I was.

IN THIS SURPRISING COLLECTION, Sammy tells about some of the most disturbing events in his life, with insights free of gloom, and full of truthful simplicity.

*Also by Susan Shreve*

ADULT
A Fortunate Madness
A Woman Like That
Children of Power

BOOKS FOR YOUNG READERS
The Nightmares of Geranium Street
Loveletters
Family Secrets

# Family Secrets

## 🍃 FIVE VERY
## IMPORTANT STORIES
## BY SUSAN SHREVE

*Illustrated by Richard Cuffari*

 *Alfred A. Knopf : New York*

*for my son Porter*
*from whom I borrow stories*

THIS IS A BORZOI BOOK PUBLISHED BY
ALFRED A. KNOPF, INC. 2/80-NEHBF-5.99/

Text copyright © 1979 by Susan Shreve
Illustrations copyright © 1979 by Alfred A. Knopf,
Inc. All rights reserved under International and
Pan-American Copyright Conventions. Published in the
United States by Alfred A. Knopf, Inc., New York,
and simultaneously in Canada by Random House of
Canada Limited, Toronto. Distributed by Random
House, Inc., New York.

Library of Congress Cataloging in Publication Data
Shreve, Susan Richards. Family secrets.
Summary: Eight-year-old Sammy tries to come to
terms with several difficult situations including the
death of his dog, the divorce of his aunt and uncle,
the suicide of his best friend's brother, coping with his
terminally ill grandmother, and cheating on a school
test. [1. Family life—Fiction] I. Title.
PZ7.S55915Fam 1979 [Fic] 78-12471
ISBN 0-394-83896-3  ISBN 0-394-93896-8 lib. bdg.

Manufactured in the United States of America
0  9  8  7  6  5  4  3  2  1

# Contents

# FAMILY SECRETS

## *1
# The Death of
# Giles

GILES DIED yesterday morning. He must have
died while I was still sleeping. After I was up and
dressed I called him to go outside, since walking the
dogs is one of my jobs in the morning. I have twice
as many jobs as anyone else in the family. When I
went into the downstairs bathroom where he sleeps
to say, "Get up, you lazy noodle, it's morning," he
was lying on the floor. I knew he was dead. Death is
different than life. It gives off a different feeling.

3

I GUESS I should have told my parents about Giles right away, but I didn't. They were still sleeping. My parents really sleep a lot—they would probably sleep all day and into the next day if I didn't wake them up to go to work. I was afraid to tell them about Giles. I am not at all sure why I was afraid. I guess I felt it might have been my fault Giles had died since I was the first one to find him like that.

I got the other children up. There are three others besides me and usually I do not want to see any of them first off in the morning. My brothers are very noisy. The baby is okay, but she has just learned to walk and is going to be a lot of trouble now. But this morning I decided to get them up. I wanted company.

I poured out bowls of Rice Krispies and even gave Philip the Zooper Looper toy. Philip is impossible! Even Mother says so. Nicholas put a whole bowl of sugar on his cereal but this time I didn't tell. I did not mention Giles and they didn't notice he wasn't

there. They didn't discover him either. After we finished our cereal I got the toys out and we played. It took forever before Daddy finally came down.

"Did you make your bed?" he asked. I always get that routine first off in the morning, but today he did say I had certainly been nice with the children. "Did you let out the dogs?"

"I let Traff out," I said. "Giles was too tired."

"Too tired?"

I watched him carefully from the corner where I sat with Nicholas and the cement mixer.

"Giley," Daddy called. He went into the bathroom where Giles slept at night. "Giley?"

He was gone a very long time and to tell you the truth, I was feeling just terrible. When he came back to the kitchen he called me and I went over. He was very quiet. He knelt down so his face was next to mine.

"Giles is dead," he said.

"I know." He didn't ask me why I hadn't told him.

Together we went up to tell Mother. She cried. My mother isn't one of those mothers who cries a lot, but sometimes she has a bad temper. We all cried, sitting there on Mother and Daddy's bed. Then I got Traff, our other dog, a very old sheepdog. I knew he was probably feeling very sad. He and Giles had been best friends for years.

Daddy took Giles to the veterinarian to find out why he had died and Mommy cooked breakfast (which takes much longer than when Daddy does it). She told the other children about Giles. They did not cry. Nicholas, who is four, seemed sad but I decided they did not care very much. Mother said it was because they are innocent and do not understand. I don't know about that.

I had to go to school. Mother said I did. She did let me wait until my eyes looked better and gave me a note to Mrs. E. Angelo, my yellow-bellied teacher, who threatens to send me to the principal every day or so. I walked to school very slowly and did not think about Giles on purpose because I did

not want to cry. I did tell everyone at recess about Giles. Most of the kids were very nice and treated me okay—except for Matt the Tatt, who has been my archenemy nonstop since kindergarten. I would gladly bounce on his belly if he weren't a lot bigger than me. He teased, "Haha hahaha—Sammy's little dog is dead." Mother says children can be awful to each other and she is right.

On the way home, I thought about Giles again and I thought how surprising it was that it had been just a regular day in spite of Giles. I had done my math and reading and written a story about the Indians and eaten lunch and was walking home now down Mercer Street as I always did. I don't know what I had expected but somehow I thought that if someone close to me died, everything around me would stop.

I ALSO expected a miracle. Mother was sitting on the rocking chair holding the baby when I walked in the front door.

"Is Giles still dead?" I asked. That kind of miracle. Even before she nodded, I knew that he was. I sat on the floor beside the rocker and told her about Matt the Tatt.

THAT AFTERNOON I didn't want to play kickball with Jeffry and Tommy or dinosaurs with Allie or climb trees back by the pond. I didn't want to do any of the things I usually do in the afternoon after school. I went upstairs to my room and sat on my bed in the exact spot where Giles used to sleep every night of my life since I got that bed, and I thought about him.

Giles was an enormous black poodle. We never clipped him, so he looked like a giant bear. He was Mother's dog really. Daddy gave him to her the Christmas before I was born, but I always thought of him as my dog because he slept with me, played ball with me, and waited in the window for me to come home from school. Giles was my brother be-

fore Nicholas and Philip came along. And sometimes when Nicholas and Philip—and now Carlotta
—rolled on him and pulled his ears and stuck their
fingers in his eyes he never growled or even nipped
at them. He was a regular prince, Daddy said. I
expect that Giles understood how I sometimes felt
about the children and missed the time when there
were just the two of us. I spent all afternoon in my
room thinking of Giles and then I fell asleep. I
never—absolutely never—fall asleep in the daytime,
but Mother told me later that sometimes when you
have had a great sadness you need extra sleep.

WE BURIED Giles that night after dinner. We buried
him under a dogwood tree in our yard, next to
Snuff, a dog Mother and Daddy had before I was
born. We all put wildflowers on Giles' grave—even
Carlotta did. It made me feel better to bury him.
Then we all sat in the yard and talked about him
for a long time until Carlotta and Philip fell asleep.

We went to bed and Daddy scratched my back until he thought I was asleep. I wasn't. I couldn't get to sleep.

"Sammy?" Nicholas called after Daddy had left. Nicholas sleeps in the bottom of my bunk bed. "Are you asleep?"

"Nope," I answered.

"Me neither."

That was obvious.

"Sammy?"

"Yup."

"Will Giles ever come back again?"

"No," I answered. It made me feel terrible to tell him that.

"Where is he?"

"He is in our heart." I told him that because I had been told it a long time ago, when my grandfather died. "When someone you love dies, you keep him in your heart."

"Oh," Nicholas said and was quiet for a long time. "Can we take him out of our heart and look at him?"

"No, Nicho," I said. Mother was sure right about the children not understanding. "We keep our memory of him in our heart."

"Oh," Nicholas said. "Sammy?" he called again. "Do you think you could sleep with me?"

Ordinarily the very *last* thing in the world I want to do is sleep with Nicholas because he always, without fail, wets the bed. But this night I climbed down the bunk ladder and crawled under the sheet with him.

"Sure," I said. "I'll sleep with you."

# ✐ 2
# At Sammy's House

I ASKED my father last night if he thought he was going to get divorced and he said no, at least not in the next two or three weeks, because he was busy with other things. Which wasn't exactly the answer I wanted.

So I asked my mother, who was doing the dishes and not good-tempered. She said of course she was getting a divorce—maybe even in the next fifteen minutes if Daddy was sitting in the living room reading the sports page. Which is just what he was doing. But that wasn't the answer I wanted either.

I'VE BEEN thinking about divorce a lot lately. I'd be crazy not to. About half my friends' parents are divorced or separated or something, which means that on weekends they have to go see their father or their mother and we can't do our regular things together. But I really started thinking a lot about divorce a few weeks ago when Aunt Margie, my father's sister, and Uncle Jake announced that they were getting a divorce. They said it right at our dinner table with their kids around looking perfectly normal, in fact, not even much interested.

My mother said their children probably knew about it long ago and maybe were even glad, because Margie and Jake fought like rats. Which is strange, because they always seemed okay around me. And now Jamie will get to see his father on weekends. When they lived in the same house, his father was never there. At least that's the way Jamie told it to me when we went up to my room after supper.

He didn't seem to mind about the divorce at all.

In fact, he got the Monopoly game down and we played along as if it was a regular thing for parents to get divorced, which I guess it is if they're not your parents. When I finally got up enough nerve to ask him how come, he didn't mind my asking and told me that Jake had found a girl friend and liked her better than Margie. If my father did that, I'd run away. I'd probably go to Alaska. I might take Nicho with me since he's okay company when he's not whining. Besides, sometimes I think my parents like Nicholas better than me. At least he gets away with more. So if I ever ran away, I'd take Nicho to make *sure* my father felt plenty sad about his new girl friend.

Jamie looked at me like I was crazy when I asked him why he didn't run away and take Lucinda, who's his sister.

"Take Lucinda!" he said. "You gotta be out of your mind."

I guess it never occurred to Jamie to run away in the first place.

"Dad was never home anyway," Jamie said matter-of-factly. "So the only difference now is his clothes aren't there either."

LATER Jamie told me that his mother was better-tempered after Jake left for good. She used to sit in her room and cry a lot and forget to start dinner and do the laundry, and Jamie and Lucinda had to do all those things for themselves. Now, since she got a job and a boy friend who was okay—only bald —and came over for dinner a lot, she cooked really good dinners again. Anyway, Jamie said if things ever got bad with his mother, he could always move in with his father for a few days and that would be great.

Well that wasn't my idea of "great." Later my mother told me it probably wasn't Jamie's idea either. He and Lucinda simply had to make the best of it.

Mother's always saying we have to make the

best of bad things. My idea is not to have bad things in the first place.

WE USED to do everything with Uncle Jake and Aunt Margie when we were small, so Jamie was like a brother to me. We went on vacations together and had Christmas together and Thanksgiving and went camping in the Shenandoah. It just kills me that I never knew anything was the matter. I must be dumber than I think.

Jamie knew. He told me one night when he stayed overnight with us that for years his father had girl friends. And finally he found one he liked well enough to live with. And he said he knew his mother really hadn't loved his father for a long time but she didn't know what to do about it.

When I asked where were Jake's girl friends when we went on all those trips, Jamie looked at me like I had three heads and said they were SECRET girl friends; so I decided not to ask Jamie any more questions about the divorce, though I've got plenty to ask about.

Sometimes I can't get to sleep at night from just thinking about it. Nicho and Philip and Carlotta are lucky. They don't know about anything. Nicho's probably never worried about anything more than if he has the right number of Tonka trucks and enough peanut butter on his sandwich. I doubt the other two will ever worry—even when they get older. It's hard being the oldest. You get all the troubles.

TOMORROW NIGHT Margie and Jamie and Lucinda are coming over for dinner with Margie's new bald boy friend. Mother's cooking roast beef which we're having to impress the boy friend for Margie's sake.

Mother and Daddy are mad at Jake about the divorce so it's pretty unlikely he'll ever be over for roast beef with his new girl friend.

It's not going to be the same though. Not at

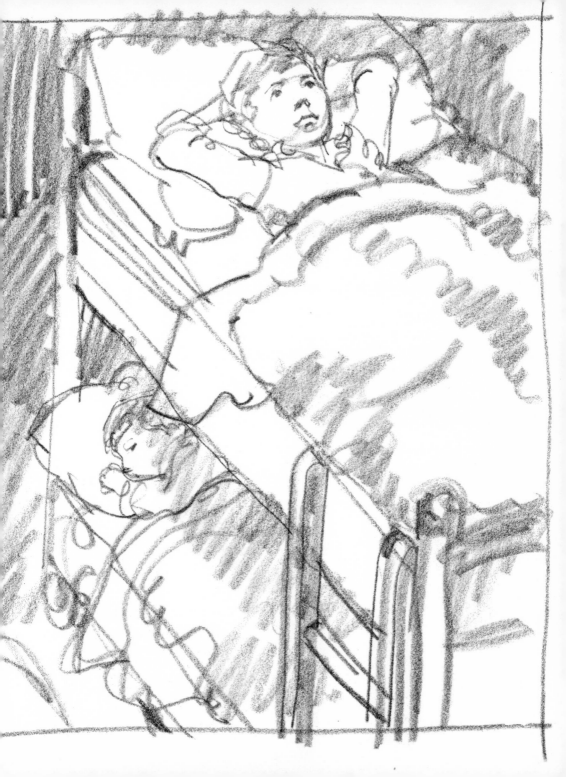

Christmas or Thanksgiving, and the bald boy friend probably hates camping in the Shenandoah. I never thought Uncle Jake was the greatest person in the world but it's kind of like someone dying to have him gone.

TONIGHT WHEN Mother came in to kiss me good night, she said she was sorry she and Daddy had teased me earlier when I asked about divorce and would I like to talk about it now.

I shrugged and said I guessed I would, not wanting to seem too interested.

So we sat and talked on my bed in the dark for a long time.

They asked me if I really thought they might get a divorce since kids just seem to know those things long before they happen. I had to admit I didn't think they would. We talked a lot about Jake and Margie—and about Mother and Daddy, too. Then I decided to sort of firm things up so I could stop worrying absolutely. I asked them if they'd promise me not to get a divorce ever.

Well, they wouldn't do that.

They said you can't promise absolutely about things in the future because certain things happen that you just don't plan for—but that it was very unlikely and that they both loved me, which was first off what mattered and always would, even if I did terrible things like throw toilet paper in the boys' bathroom or drink Cokes all day. So I went to sleep and didn't have bad dreams that night for a change.

# ॐ 3
# Willy's Brother

THE MOVERS came to the Henrys' house today and took out everything. Nicholas and I sat on the bank in front of our house to watch.

They took the Ping-Pong table where Willy used to beat me regularly until last year when I grew five inches in two months—and the kitchen table where I ate a hundred lunches or more from the time I was old enough to cross the Henrys' driveway by myself—and the paintings of the children which used to hang over the mantle in the living room, all painted when they were five years old.

There was Willy at five years old, and Eric who's eleven now and the Little League pitcher for the team that won last summer. And finally, Michael, who hanged himself in the Henrys' basement four weeks ago Friday.

THE MORNING after Michael died, the Henrys left to stay at Mrs. Henry's family home in Massachusetts. They just took Willy and Eric out of school and left and sold their house saying they couldn't live there again because of Michael. They've moved to a different part of town, so I won't get to see Willy anymore unless we make arrangements and that's just not the same.

I haven't seen him since the afternoon before Michael died when Willy and I went down to Zuckers and had ice cream and bought baseball cards. It was then that Willy told me his parents were taking everyone in the family on a trip to Gettysburg except Michael, who had had a fight with his father and had locked himself in his room. Looking back, Willy didn't seem worried much. He was always saying Michael was strange, and I'd say he seemed pretty regular to me, and then Willy'd say that's cause I didn't live with him and Eric. Which could be true. I think Nicholas is strange—and Philip and Carlotta, too, off and on. But mostly Nicholas.

THE NEXT THING we knew of Michael, he was dead. His mother found him in the basement Saturday night. The television people came to our house while I was doing math, because Mr. Henry's famous around town and it was a big deal that his son died. Only my parents wouldn't talk to the television people. My father even told them it was none of their business to make television shows of real people's sadness, but they did it anyway and he watched it on the ten o'clock news after Nicholas, Carlotta, Philip, and I were in bed. My mother didn't go to bed but she wouldn't watch. Mrs. Henry was her good friend and Michael, too, I guess, though later we found out Michael didn't think he had any good friends.

WE ALL looked up to Michael Henry like he was something special—which he was. He was the fastest runner in the high school even though he was only a junior and he got the book prize for good grades every year running according to Willy, who didn't think it was so much of a big deal. Everyone around said he'd probably be famous like his father, who was a lawyer but not a regular lawyer like some fathers. Michael seemed to think so, too, because he never talked to the rest of us ordinary kids. We didn't talk to him much either.

In fact, the only time I ever did talk to Michael Henry was by accident. I was in his room looking at all his trophies, which just about filled the place up, when he came in and sat down on his bed without my even noticing or I would've gotten out fast since he was six years older than me and twice my size—not counting being famous. Anyhow, he sat on the bed and asked me if Willy was my best friend.

I nodded because mostly it was true, except the time he broke my AI rifle.

Then he asked me what we talked about.

The truth is Willy and I don't talk much. We play. But I had to say something so I said we talked about the bad teachers, our enemies in fifth grade, and some other things like that.

Then he asked me why I thought Willy and Eric had so many friends. Well, it had never occurred to me that they had *so* many friends. We all have about the same number of friends and enemies, give or take a couple. But I said it was because they were good guys most of the time. Then I started to leave.

The thing was I wanted to get out of Michael's room since I didn't know what to say to someone that old and well known in our town.

So when he asked me another question, I pretended not to hear.

Now, of course, I feel terrible about it.

I WAS DOING my homework on Saturday night so I could go to the circus the next day with Willy and my other friend, when I heard a terrible sound outside my bedroom window. Later I found out it was Mrs. Henry—I call her Aunt Dorsey—and she'd just discovered Michael. I listened from my room, then I ran downstairs. By that time my parents knew what was up and they told me Michael was dead. My mother let me forget my homework and said I had to go to bed right away. Well, you can imagine, I didn't go to sleep right away. There was noise and talking and people going in and out all night, but I didn't creep out of bed. I thought if boys like Michael could die just as easy as that, I'd better stay put where I was. I only found out the next day what really happened.

EVERYBODY IN THE neighborhood and a bunch of people I'd never seen before were in front of the Henrys' the next afternoon.

Mr. Havelton, who lives next door, on the other side of us, was telling the reporters about Michael—about how he was the most perfectly normal regular boy and how he won everything and had millions of friends and liked his parents and what can you make of a world where boys like that want to kill themselves.

Later my father told me it wasn't true about Michael being very happy one minute and dead the next. He must have been very unhappy and lonely to have wanted to die. We just didn't know about it.

Of course, I thought about that time in Michael's room when I pretended not to hear him. Upstairs that afternoon doing my homework, since we never did go to the circus after all, I began to think about Michael deciding he was going to die and wondered whether he was thinking about how I'd let him down.

I got plenty lonely then, so I went downstairs where Carlotta and Philip were spreading peanut butter all over the table. My father was looking out the kitchen window as if there was a regular side-show in the backyard and peanut buttering the table was something we did every day.

I decided to tell my father how Michael's dying was probably my fault. He said we always feel like that, especially when someone dies the way Michael did.

"It's nobody's fault," he said. "We didn't know and the Henrys didn't know how lonely Michael was. Michael didn't tell anyone. If he had, someone would have been able to help him."

Then my father said it was a good thing I'd come downstairs and told him I felt terrible because now we could talk about it. That didn't mean I'd feel fine afterward but at least I wouldn't feel lonely. Which was true. I didn't feel fine, but I didn't feel lonely either.

Later, when Mary Dawson and Terry Burns

came over and we got to talking about whether we'd kill ourselves when we got older, I told them what my father had said and we made a pact right there to be firm friends and always help each other out in trouble.

THE MOVING VAN MEN slammed the doors of the truck and pulled away. I watched it go all the way down Mercer.

"Have they gone?" my father asked.

"Yup," I said, feeling pretty much like crying but not.

"Then let's go call Willy," he said.

My heart gave a jump. I hadn't seen Willy in a month and I'd pretty much given up on seeing him again.

"For what?"

"To come over," my father said. "We'll all go out to Taylor Park for a picnic. Willy's probably feeling rotten."

"Yeah," I said. I remembered how we used to play catch in the Henrys' driveway or lay for hours under their apple tree playing with our model cars, how we went to school together every day taking the short cut through the Marlands' yard to avoid our first-rate enemies on Mercer Street. I wondered if Willy thought about Michael like I do every night lately. I even keep a night light on now, like Nicho.

"D'you think Willy wants to see me?" I asked cautiously.

"Of course," my father said. "I'm sure he's been waiting to hear from you for a long time."

"D'you think he's changed?" I asked. "You know. Since Michael."

"He's changed," my father said to me. "You've changed since Michael, too. We all have."

"I guess," I said, thinking suddenly of Willy in a new house and a new school with no friends and maybe having bad dreams. "He'll probably want me to bring my baseball glove and stuff," I said, going into the house after my father.

# 4
# Grandmama Welty

I NEVER thought much about how Grandmama Welty looked until my new friend Amos came over the first time, took one look at her sitting on the living room couch where she's sat all day for six months, and bolted.

I found him walking down Mercer Street at a clip and had to run to catch up with him.

"What happened?" I asked.

"She's old," he said and you could tell he was scared.

"Haven't you ever seen anybody old before?"

"Not that old," he said.

The thing is, she's not that old. I have a great-grandmother who's ninety-five and everybody admits that's pretty old, but Grandmama Welty was only seventy on Wednesday. So it's not how old she is.

"And she looks terrible," Amos added.

Which I had to admit was true.

I don't bother about Grandmama's looks because she's just there sitting on the couch all day and I've gotten used to her, but after Amos bolted, I made a picture of Grandmama in my mind—pretending I was Amos—and what I saw was pretty bad.

First off, she shakes. Even her face shakes, one side of it especially. "Palsy," my mother calls it and there's nothing you can do about it.

"Except drink," Mother shouted one night at Daddy loud enough for Grandmama, who was sitting on the couch, to hear. "Your mother had so much to drink tonight, Sammy had to take her from the table."

I did. And when I sat her down on the couch, she was asleep with her mouth open so you could see where her teeth are gone.

EVER SINCE Grandmama came to live with us last Christmas—she came for Christmas and never went home—she drinks anything she can find, and lately it's bottles and bottles of Vicks 44 cough syrup. I myself am sent out to buy her two bottles every afternoon when I come home from school. I think my father gets her real liquor and sneaks it to her because I saw him slip a bottle in the bottom of the record-player cabinet once. She's his mother and he feels awful about her.

"So what if she drinks?" he said one night to my mother. "She's in terrible pain."

"I know," my mother agreed.

But a couple of times I've come home from school to find Mother in the kitchen slamming plates and pans in such a temper I try to sneak out again.

"Your grandmother will outlive me," she said once, but I could tell she didn't mean it.

Grandmama has cancer and she's probably not going to outlive anybody. When she came to visit us at Christmas time, Daddy said she had to see a doctor because she looked like she was dead already with nothing but skeleton left of her. Every time she smoked a cigarette—which was about twenty times a day—she dropped it on the floor and Mother said it was pretty likely we'd all burn up if Daddy didn't do something about his mother. It's always *his* mother when Mommy's mad.

GRANDMAMA WENT to the hospital for the first time, the first time for her since all her children were born at home, and had an operation. The doctor said there was nothing he could do—she had cancer all over and that was that.

Of course we decided she should stay at our house because she hates hospitals. Besides, she doesn't even

think she's sick. Or at least she pretends pretty well.

If anybody asks her how she feels, she says just fine. Once in plain desperation, because it's sometimes hard on my mother to have her around, Mother asked her wouldn't she be happier in a nursing home where Nicho wasn't stepping on her toes and Carlotta crawling all over her—and Grandmama just said maybe so when she got old and weak.

Mommy and I gave each other these looks when she said that because no one we know is weaker than Grandmama.

She doesn't complain. Philip even runs over her toes with Tonka trucks. (I mean, that's the kind of brothers I've got—can you imagine being that stupid!) But if it weren't for that she wouldn't complain at all, although she coughs all day long, even when she's sleeping.

I talk to her sometimes in the afternoon when I come home from school. She talks about my father when he was small, and the way she remembers it, he was a regular hero, but Daddy says her memory is bad. I expect he was okay, though, even great sometimes. She doesn't talk much about us. In fact she keeps forgetting Nicho and Carlotta's names. She never forgets my name. But she shouldn't because I was named for her husband.

"I don't think she knows we're around," my mother said to my father one night. "She can't even remember my name."

Sometimes she calls my mother Maggie, which really makes my mother hot-fired angry because Maggie's the name of my father's old girl friend.

"Is she getting to be too much trouble for you?" my father asked my mother.

I thought she was going to say yes, but she didn't. I was really proud of her because I can tell it's trouble, especially the nights Grandmama's had so much to drink that she keeps putting a match to the wrong end of the cigarette and it smells bad. Once she caught the wastebasket in the living room on fire. That time Mother didn't say a word. Just put out the fire with a hose from the backyard and hid Grandmama's cigarettes. But for all that cancer, Grandmama's pretty smart and she found them again.

ONE NIGHT Nicho and I were looking at the photograph album. There were some pictures in it of Grandmama when she was young. I can't tell you how pretty she was. It was hard to believe those pictures were of the same person sitting on the couch.

"D'you think you'll get to look like Grandmama?" I asked my mother—who I think is the prettiest woman I know, even if she is getting wrinkles.

"Maybe," Mother said. "Not for a while though."

"Do people like you better when you're young?" I asked. I wanted to know because I'd been thinking I really didn't much like to kiss Grandmama and things like that.

"I guess they do but they shouldn't," Mother said. "We all get old. You will, and Nicho and me, everyone. And we should like each other just as much. Grandmama's a little like Carlotta in a way—only less trouble."

That was something for my mother to say. She thinks Carlotta is first-rate 'cause she's a girl—and for a first-rate girl, Carlotta is plenty of trouble.

That night, we took the photograph album down and looked at it with Grandmama and she told us funny stories about all the people in it—especially my grandfather and my father. We had a good time. She had the best time of all.

That night when my father tucked me into bed he thanked me for being so nice to Grandmama— which was crazy because we all had the best time without even trying.

I THOUGHT about all these things after I caught up with my new friend Amos, and I even told him a

couple of the funny stories. And he said how about if we went over to *his* house to play instead.

I said no, because I knew the only reason he wouldn't come to *my* house was 'cause he thought Grandmama was creepy and he didn't want to have to see her.

So he said he'd just decided he didn't want to come to my house today. Maybe some other time. I said that was just fine and went home and played gin rummy with Grandmama. She beat me two times running.

# 5
# Cheating

I CHEATED on a unit test in math class this morning during second period with Mr. Burke. Afterward, I was too sick to eat lunch just thinking about it.

I came straight home from school, went to my room, and lay on the floor trying to decide whether it would be better to run away from home now or after supper. Mostly I wished I was dead.

IT WASN'T even an accident that I cheated.

Yesterday Mr. Burke announced there'd be a

unit test and anyone who didn't pass would have to come to school on Saturday, most particularly me, since I didn't pass the last unit test. He said that right out in front of everyone as usual. You can imagine how much I like Mr. Burke.

But I did plan to study just to prove to him that I'm plenty smart—which I am mostly—except in math, which I'd be okay in if I'd memorize my times tables. Anyway, I got my desk ready to study on since it was stacked with about two million things. Just when I was ready to work, Nicho came into my room with our new rabbit and it jumped on my desk and knocked the flash cards all over the floor.

I yelled for my mother to come and help me pick them up, but Carlotta was crying as usual and Mother said I was old enough to help myself and a bunch of other stuff like that which mothers like to say. My mother's one of those people who tells you everything you've done wrong for thirty years like you do it every day. It drives me crazy.

Anyway, Nicho and I took the rabbit outside but then Philip came to my room and also Marty from next door and before long it was dinner. After dinner my father said I could watch a special on television if I'd done all my homework.

Of course I said I had.

That was the beginning. I felt terrible telling my father a lie about the homework so I couldn't even enjoy the special. I guessed he knew I was lying and was so disappointed he couldn't talk about it.

Not much is important in our family. Marty's mother wants him to look okay all the time and my friend Nathan has to do well in school and Andy has so many rules he must go crazy just trying to remember them. My parents don't bother making up a lot of rules. But we do have to tell the truth—even if it's bad, which it usually is. You can imagine how I didn't really enjoy the special.

It was nine o'clock when I got up to my room and that was too late to study for the unit test so

I lay in my bed with the light off and decided what I would do the next day when I was in Mr. B.'s math class not knowing the 8- and 9-times tables.

So, you see, the cheating was planned after all.

But at night, thinking about Mr. B.—who could scare just about anybody I know, even my father— it seemed perfectly sensible to cheat. It didn't even seem bad when I thought of my parents' big thing about telling the truth.

I'd go into class jolly as usual, acting like things were going just great, and no one, not even Mr. B., would suspect the truth. I'd sit down next to Stanley Plummer—he is so smart in math it makes you sick—and from time to time, I'd glance over at his paper to copy the answers. It would be a cinch. In fact, every test before, I had to try hard not to see his answers because our desks are practically on top of each other.

And that's exactly what I did this morning. It was a cinch. Everything was okay except that my stomach was upside down and I wanted to die.

THE FACT IS, I couldn't believe what I'd done in cold blood. I began to wonder about myself—really wonder—things like whether I would steal from stores or hurt someone on purpose or do some other terrible thing I couldn't even imagine. I began to wonder whether I was plain bad to the core.

I've never been a wonderful kid that everybody in the world loves and thinks is swell, like Nicho. I have a bad temper and I like to have my own way and I argue a lot. Sometimes I can be mean. But most of the time I've thought of myself as a pretty decent kid. Mostly I work hard, I stick up for little kids, and I tell the truth. Mostly I like myself fine—except I wish I were better at basketball.

Now all of a sudden I've turned into this criminal. It's hard to believe I'm just a boy. And all because of one stupid math test.

Lying on the floor of my room, I begin to think that probably I've been bad all along. It just took this math test to clinch it. I'll probably never tell the truth again.

I tell my mother I'm sick when she calls me to come down for dinner. She doesn't believe me, but puts me to bed anyhow. I lie there in the early winter darkness wondering what terrible thing I'll be doing next when my father comes in and sits down on my bed.

"What's the matter?" he asks.

"I've got a stomachache," I say. Luckily, it's too dark to see his face.

"Is that all?"

"Yeah."

"Mommy says you've been in your room since school."

"I was sick there, too," I say.

"She thinks something happened today and you're upset."

That's the thing that really drives me crazy about my mother. She knows things sitting inside my head same as if I was turned inside out.

"Well," my father says. I can tell he doesn't believe me.

"My stomach *is* feeling sort of upset." I hedge.

"Okay," he says and he pats my leg and gets up.

Just as he shuts the door to my room I call out to him in a voice I don't even recognize as my own that I'm going to have to run away.

"How come?" he calls back not surprised or anything.

So I tell him I cheated on this math test. To tell the truth, I'm pretty much surprised at myself. I didn't plan to tell him anything.

He doesn't say anything at first and that just about kills me. I'd be fine if he'd spank me or something. To say nothing can drive a person crazy.

And then he says I'll have to call Mr. Burke.

It's not what *I* had in mind.

"Now?" I ask surprised.

"Now," he says. He turns on the light and pulls off my covers.

"I'm not going to," I say.

But I do it. I call Mr. Burke, probably waking him up, and I tell him exactly what happened, even that I decided to cheat the night before the test. He says I'll come in Saturday to take another test, which is okay with me, and I thank him a whole lot for being understanding and all. He's not friendly but he's not absolutely mean either.

"Today I thought I was turning into a criminal," I tell my father when he turns out my light.

Sometimes my father kisses me good night and sometimes he doesn't. I never know. But tonight he does.

SUSAN SHREVE is the author of two other books for young people, *The Nightmares of Geranium Street* and *Loveletters,* both published by Knopf. Her adult novels include *A Fortunate Madness* and *A Woman Like That* (an ALA Notable Book, 1977).

Susan Shreve, a graduate of the University of Pennsylvania, is currently an assistant professor of English at George Mason University.

Ms. Shreve, her husband, and their four children live in Washington, D.C. The stories in this collection were originally written as a gift for her eldest child.

# IN MEMORIAM

RICHARD CUFFARI (1925-1978) whose sensitive drawings of children and adults are well-known and widely-admired, has illustrated numerous children's books over the years.

*Family Secrets* was Richard Cuffari's last work in progress with Knopf. As a tribute to him, we are publishing his final sketches for the book's inside drawings. The jacket art—a portrait of the book's main character—is a composite drawing of the artist's own four children.